Everyone is SMART

NOOR ABDELRAHMAN

Noor Abdelrahm

January, 2023

Wasteland Press
www.wastelandpress.net
Shelbyville, KY USA

Everyone is Smart
by Noor Abdelrahman

Copyright © 2015 Noor Abdelrahman
ALL RIGHTS RESERVED

First Printing – December 2015
ISBN: 978-1-68111-083-7

Printed in the U.S.A.

0 1 2

For Anan and Zaina, and all my students –
who are smart and special **each** *in their own way.*

– N.A.

Zaina loved going to school.
She loved learning and wanted to be the best at
EVERYTHING!

Her favorite subject was reading.
She read night and day.
Her head was always stuck in a book.

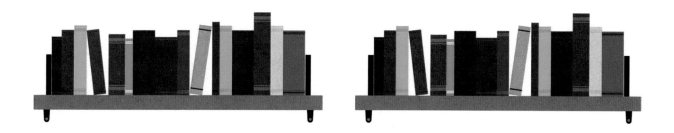

She also enjoyed writing.

She wrote stories all the time and shared them with her friends.

She even liked science and didn't mind getting her hands dirty once in a while.

But there was one subject Zaina did not like...

MATH

Her stomach always turned in knots when it was time for math.

She practiced and practiced but never seemed to understand.

She spent hours on her homework and made lots of mistakes.

Zaina always tried her best, but math was just too difficult.

One particular day at school, Zaina's stomach was in bigger knots than usual.

"I will be returning your math quizzes from yesterday," her teacher Ms. Connor announced. Zaina immediately felt her heart racing in her chest. She was not looking forward to the results.

Ms. Connor picked up the stack of papers from her desk and began circulating the classroom. "Great job! Keep up the good work," she said with a smile.

Zaina continued to fret as her teacher walked toward her. She stopped in front of Zaina's desk, placed the quiz face down, sighed, and turned away without saying a word.

Zaina paused for a moment before she slowly lifted up the quiz. She took a quick peek, but all she could see were red pen marks. She folded the paper in half and quickly hid it in her backpack. As soon as the class was dismissed, Zaina rushed out of the room to avoid seeing or speaking to anyone.

When Zaina was halfway down the hall, she heard her best friend Lilly call out. Zaina could see Lilly heading her way from the corner of her eye. She turned around to face Lilly, who was grinning from ear to ear. She was very good at math and always did well.

"How did you do on the math quiz?" Lilly asked excitedly. "Umm, I did okay," mumbled Zaina in almost a whisper. Zaina didn't even bother to ask Lilly about her score. It just would have made her feel worse.

"I'm glad to hear that!" replied Lilly enthusiastically. "Well, I'll see you tomorrow. Good luck on Friday's test!" said Lilly as she walked down the hall and disappeared into the crowd of students.

Zaina froze. She completely forgot about the test. Her teacher had been talking about it for days. *How did I forget?* She thought. *It's okay. Don't panic,* she told herself. *I have plenty of time to study. I will get a fresh start tonight and practice extra hard.* Zaina was determined to get a perfect score this time.

That evening, Zaina did not have time to write or read her favorite stories. Instead, she stayed in her room and studied for hours. Getting a perfect math grade was far more important than anything else.

The following day, she went directly home again. This time she missed soccer practice. She was still too concerned about the math test. She studied even harder than the night before and stayed up extra late. Although Zaina was exhausted, she felt confident and fully prepared.

On Friday afternoon, Zaina sat at her desk anxiously waiting. She picked up her pencil the second she heard Ms. Connor say "Begin." She solved the first few problems instantly without any trouble. Zaina was on a roll and off to a good start.

As Zaina made her way near the end of the test, she came across a big problem-solving question. She reread the question several times but didn't quite get it. She tried to concentrate, but all she could hear was the sound of rattling papers and scratching pencils. Suddenly, she felt the knots in her stomach return. She looked down at the test which now appeared to be nothing but a big blur. Zaina sulked in her chair and stared blankly at the page.

She completely lost track of time and unexpectedly heard the dismissal bell. Her classmates handed in their tests as they quickly filed out of the room. Zaina, on the other hand, remained seated with her head down.

Ms. Connor stood up from her desk and quietly approached Zaina. "Is something wrong?" she asked. Zaina looked up at her teacher with a tear rolling down her cheek.

"I just don't get it," cried Zaina with anger and frustration. "Math is too hard because I'm not smart enough," she blurted out.

"Oh Zaina, that's not true at all," said Ms. Connor. "You don't have to be perfect to be smart. Everyone struggles with something. We all learn differently and are good at different subjects."

"What do you mean?" asked Zaina as she slowly raised her head and gently wiped away her tears.

"There are many ways to be smart," continued her teacher. "I know that you are very good at reading, writing, and vocabulary words. That means you are **word smart**."

"I never realized that," responded Zaina. She thought long and hard about what her teacher had explained. Then she began to think about all the people she knew and what they were good at.

MUSIC SMART

She thought of her friend Sammy who was great at singing and playing musical instruments.

LOGIC SMART

Her best friend Lilly was really good at solving math problems, puzzles, and working with all sorts of numbers.

PICTURE SMART

She remembered her classmate Michael. He was an excellent artist who loved drawing, painting, and using his imagination.

BODY SMART

Her brother Anan was very active and liked to move around. He was an awesome athlete who could play almost any sport.

NATURE SMART

Mr. Andrews, her science teacher, enjoyed being outdoors. He knew a lot about nature, animals, and the environment.

PEOPLE SMART

Her cousin Lana was good at socializing and talking to people. She worked well in groups and got along with just about everyone.

SELF SMART

Her next door neighbor Jenna liked to be alone sometimes and knew a lot about herself.

Zaina felt better already and continued to consider what Ms. Connor had taught her.

She went home that day without any knots in her stomach. She decided never to stress as long as she tries her best.

After all, nobody is perfect.

Everyone is smart and special in his or her own way.

WORD SMART	BODY SMART
MUSIC SMART	NATURE SMART
LOGIC SMART	PEOPLE SMART
PICTURE SMART	SELF SMART

ABOUT THE AUTHOR

Noor Abdelrahman has a passion for writing and an appreciation for children's literature. As an elementary teacher, she places a strong emphasis on both subjects in her classroom. She holds a master's degree in education. Through her graduate program, she learned the significance of Howard Gardner's Theory of Multiple Intelligences, which was the topic of her master's thesis. This book is a reflection of her studies and research that she hopes will help shape young minds.

Made in the USA
Columbia, SC
20 November 2022

71122922R00022